Rabén & Sjögren Bokförlag, Stockholm
www.raben.se

Translation copyright © 2007 by Rabén & Sjögren Bokförlag
Originally published in Sweden by Rabén & Sjögren under the title
Skrotsamlarskolan med Jonny och Antti
Text copyright © 2006 by Adam Dahlin
Pictures copyright © 2006 by Emma Åkerman
All rights reserved
Distributed in Canada by Douglas & McIntyre Ltd.
Library of Congress Control Number: 2006936525
Printed in Denmark
First American edition, 2007

ISBN-13: 978-91-29-66736-3
ISBN-10: 91-29-66736-4

*Rabén & Sjögren Bokförlag is part of
P. A. Norstedt & Söner Publishing Group, established in 1823*

Adam Dahlin   Emma Åkerman

JUNK COLLECTOR SCHOOL

Translated by Joan Sandin

R&S
BOOKS

Stockholm New York London Adelaide Toronto

The old guy's name is Jake,
and he's got to be the best neighbor in the whole world.
He has a dog named Trash,
and he always has a dollar in his pocket.
But best of all: Jake is a junk collector.
His house is full of the most amazing collections.
Andy is the little kid.
He is like most six-year-olds:
he loves dogs, dollars, and junk.
Andy doesn't collect anything special himself,
but Jake thinks he should.
"Otherwise, life can get a little meaningless,"
he says.

Andy would love to be a junk collector.
The thing is, he doesn't know
what to collect.
Jake already collects everything.

Collecting fishing poles might be fun, thinks Andy.
But Jake already has twenty-three of them in his garage.
Maybe alarm clocks . . .
Every morning, forty-three of them ring at Jake's house.
Then how about labels from old soda bottles . . .
Jake already has five albums full.

Or empty toilet paper rolls . . .
But Jake has collected empty
toilet paper rolls since 1983.
"Someday there will be a market for them,
and I'll be a millionaire," Jake likes to say.

He already collects everything cool.
It feels like nothing's left over for Andy.

"The thing is, you lack an education," says Jake one day.
"Without a degree from Junk Collector School
you haven't got a chance."

Andy would love to go to a school
where he would learn to be a junk collector.
That's why today he is so unbelievably lucky,
because classes are starting in five minutes.
"But it will cost you five empty toilet paper rolls," says Jake.
"No problem," says Andy. "Let's go!"

As soon as they get to the big woods, Jake says,
"Rule number one: A collection shall be made up
of the same kind of stuff."
Trash finds some sticks for her collection.

Wouldn't you know!
Everybody collects something.
Everybody except me, Andy thinks.

Beside a brook, Andy finds an old blow-up crocodile!
What luck! Now, that's the kind of thing he could collect.

Jake thinks it's a good idea, too.
"I'll teach you all about crocodile collecting," he says.
Jake lets Trash smell the plastic crocodile.
"Now she'll sniff out every single crocodile for miles around," says Jake.
"Fetch, Trash, fetch crocodiles!"

Trash takes off like a rocket.
When she finally comes back,
her mouth is stuffed with sticks.

They keep on searching for a long time,
but there are no more crocodiles in these woods.
"One crocodile isn't much of a collection,"sighs Andy.
So they keep on walking.

"RULE NUMBER TWO: Always check out garbage cans.
People throw away the most fantastic stuff," explains Jake.
"RULE NUMBER THREE: Jump down inside and search thoroughly."
Jake disappears into the garbage can.

After a little while, he pops up again, filthy, but very proud of himself.
"In this garbage can I have discovered
no fewer than ten Popsicle sticks,
some bicycle handlebars,
four plastic bottles,
and a half-eaten hamburger.

"Is there anything here you'd like to start collecting?
If not, I'll gladly take the handlebars."
Andy thinks the Popsicle sticks are cool,
but Trash snatches them first.
Of course she does.
She wants them for her stick collection.

Andy still doesn't have anything to collect.
But wait—what are those shiny things behind the garbage can?

"What a find!"
Right next to the can there are two lawn mowers.
"RULE NUMBER FOUR: Collect only things that are
unusual, beautiful, and valuable," says Jake.
Somebody must have tried to throw them away
and, when they wouldn't fit in the garbage can,
just left them sitting next to it.
Now Andy has his own collection.
Finally!

They start pushing the lawn mowers home.
"Stop, thieves!"
Andy and Jake look around,
but they don't see thieves anywhere,
just two guys running toward them.
"You can't steal our lawn mowers!
How would we play soccer if you did that?"
Jake explains they had only meant to
help them cut the grass.

While Jake mows the soccer field,
Andy continues looking for something to collect.
He finds a big metal barrel,
but he knows he'll never find another one like it.
It's hopeless!
"RULE NUMBER FIVE: Don't give up; it's always hardest
in the beginning," hollers Jake as he comes roaring by with
the lawn mower.
"Your ship will come in. Just stick with me."
My ship will come in . . . That's it!
Andy has an idea!

First he runs back to the garbage can next to the big field.
What luck! The plastic bottles are still there.

Then back to the little brook in the big woods.
Lucky again! The crocodile is also still there.

"My new collection is almost finished!" Andy laughs.
"A collection shall be made up of the same kind of stuff.
That is the first rule. Have you already forgotten it?" asks Jake.
"But all of this stuff *is* the same," Andy answers.
"Don't you see that?"

Jake finds an empty can.
"Does this belong in your collection?"
"Definitely not," answers Andy.
Jake picks up a rusty bike.
"Does this belong in your collection, then?"
"No, but the tires would if they didn't have holes," says Andy.
"You're too young to truly understand collecting. I should have
known that from the beginning," says Jake.

When they get home, Andy locks himself
in the boathouse.
Jake hangs around outside.
"RULE NUMBER SIX: A junk collector doesn't
forget to eat. And now I'm going to thaw out a whole bag
of Gummy Bears—enough for you, me, and Trash."
But Andy isn't listening.
"RULE NUMBER SEVEN: Listen to your neighbor!"
says Jake.

Soon Jake hears slamming and banging from inside
the boathouse, but he isn't curious.
Not at all.
There just happen to be some wild strawberries
growing under the window. Otherwise, he would never
sneak around the boathouse like he was spying on Andy
and his weird collection.
Hardly.
Jake is only interested in the wild strawberries.

Finally, Andy opens the door.
"What are you doing? Why don't you help me
instead? This needs to be launched," he says.
"What needs to be launched? This pile of garbage?" asks Jake.
"Don't you see?" says Andy.
The only thing Jake sees is a bunch of junk all nailed together.

"A raft! Well, you could have said so, because that is just
what I thought it was from the beginning," says Jake.

Andy and Trash are anxious to take the first voyage,
but Jake stops them.
"First we have to make a speech,
and drink a whole bottle of soda,
and fire off some rockets," he says.
"That's the way you do a launch."
He starts with the speech:

"Dearest pile of junk!
You are made up of all sorts of stuff, all of which floats.
And the same kind of stuff put together makes a collection.
Therefore you are no pile of junk.
You are a collection. A collection that floats.
Just as I thought from the beginning . . ."

Andy had never floated on a raft before.
But Jake had.
Lots of times, in fact.
And Andy is really in luck today because Jake's rafting school
is going to start in just five minutes, and Andy's welcome
to join if he wants to.
But it will cost five empty toilet paper rolls.
"No problem," says Andy. "Let's go!"

"LESSON NUMBER ONE: Lie completely still
and just look up at the sky," says Jake.